# BBC DOCTOR WHO

## is for TARDIS

Illustrated by
## Adam Howling

PUFFIN

# A is for

**angel**

# B is for

bow tie

# C

is for

## Cyberman

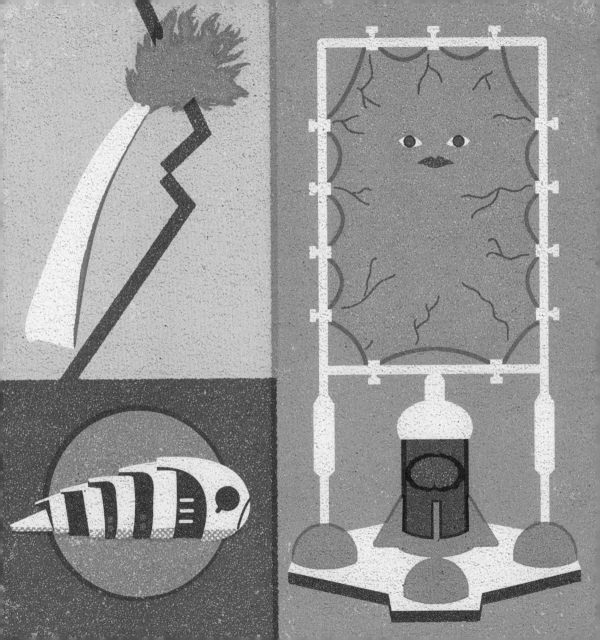

# D

is for

Doctor

E is for **Empty Child**

# F is for

## fish fingers

# G is for **Gallifrey**

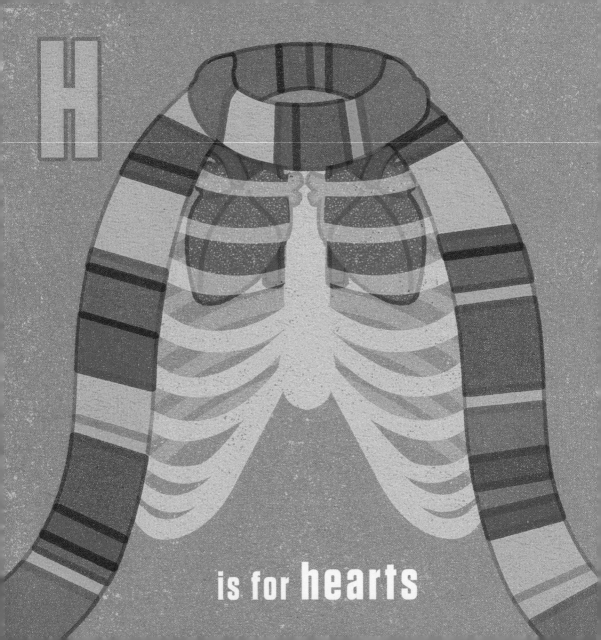

**H**

is for **hearts**

is for **impossible**

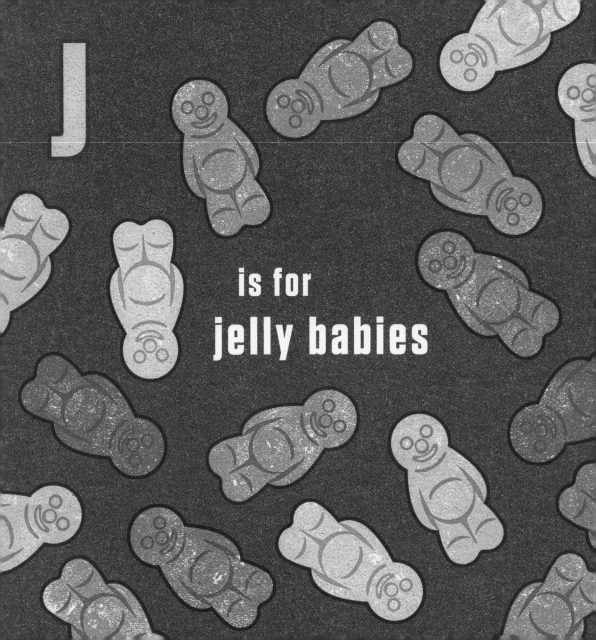

**J**

is for
**jelly babies**

**K**

is for **K-9**

is for **London**

# M is for

## Macra

**N** is for **New New York**

# P

is for

parting

# Q is for

question mark

is for **run!**

# S

## is for

Silence

**T**

is for **TARDIS**

is for **UNIT**

POLICE PUBLIC BOX

**V**

**is for vortex**

# W

is for
## warrior

X **is for**

eXterminate!

is for **allons-y!**

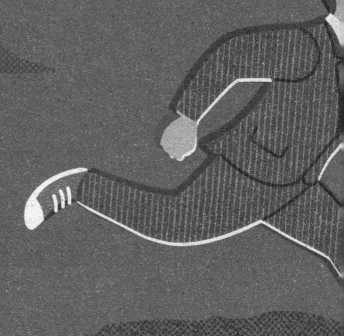

**Z** is for **Zygon**